If My Mom Were a Bird

by

Jedda Robaard

little bee books

In loving memory of my Mom.
- J.R.

little bee books

An imprint of Bonnier Publishing Group

853 Broadway, New York, New York 10003

Copyright © 2014 by Jedda Robaard. This little bee books edition 2015.

All rights reserved, including the right of reproduction in whole or in part in any form.

LITTLE BEE BOOKS is a trademark of Bonnier Publishing Group, and associated
colophon is a trademark of Bonnier Publishing Group.

Manufactured in China 1014 HH

First Edition 2 4 6 8 10 9 7 5 3 1

Library of Congress Control Number: 2014943630

ISBN 978-1-4998-0021-0

www.littlebeebooks.com
www.bonnierpublishing.com

If my mom were a bird,
she would be a tall and graceful . . .

swan

If my mom were a bird,
she would be a funny, sneaky . . .

parrot

If my mom were a bird,
she would surely be a watchful . . .

If my mom were a bird,
she would be a busy, energetic . . .

woodpecker

If my mom were a bird,
she would be a squawky, noisy . . .

canary

If my mom were a bird,
she would be a super-speedy . . .

ostrich

If my mom were a bird,
she would be a curious . . .

blue jay

If my mom were a bird,
she would be a happy . . .

chicken!

Because she's always warm and cuddly!